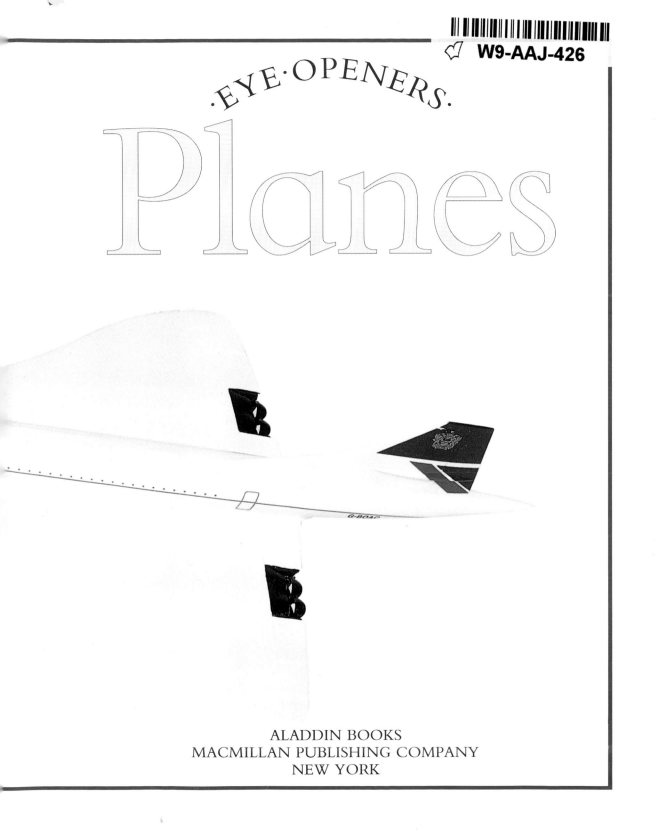

·EYE·OPENERS·

Planes

ALADDIN BOOKS
MACMILLAN PUBLISHING COMPANY
NEW YORK

W9-AAJ-426

Light aircraft

Light aircraft are small planes. They are used for many different jobs. This light aircraft helps fight forest fires. The pilot flies low over the fire and tells the fire fighters where to spray water.

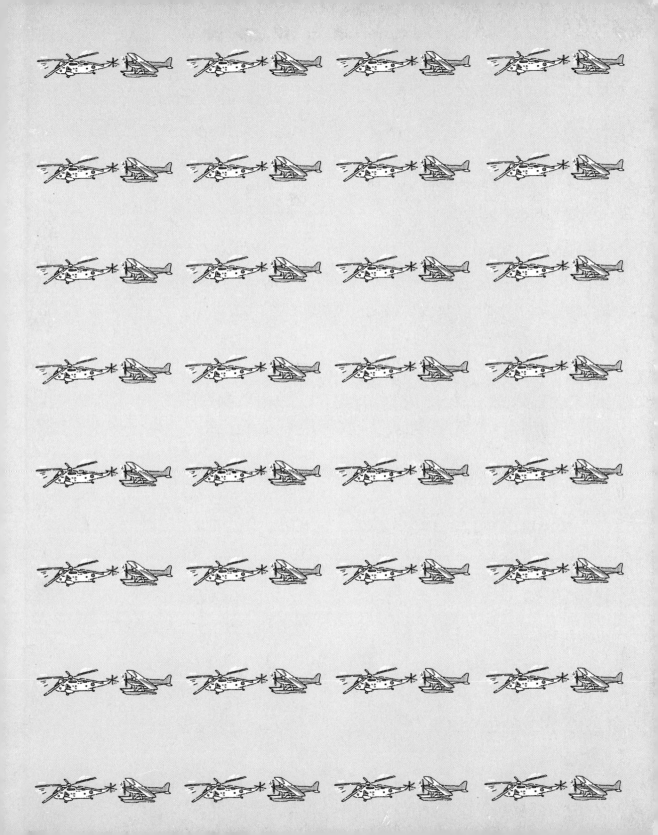

DK

A DORLING KINDERSLEY BOOK

Written by Angela Royston
Photography by Tim Ridley
Additional photography by Acorn Studios PLC, London (pages 6-7)
Illustrations by Jane Cradock-Watson and Dave Hopkins
Model makers Ted Taylor (pages 4-17 and 20-21)
and Edgar Gillingwater (pages 18-19)

Copyright © 1992 by Dorling Kindersley Limited, London

All rights reserved. No part of this book may be reproduced
or transmitted in any form or by any means, electronic or mechanical,
including photocopying, recording, or by any information storage
and retrieval system, without permission in writing from the Publisher.

BRITISH AIRWAYS

Aladdin Books
Macmillan Publishing Company
866 Third Avenue
New York, NY 10022

Macmillan Publishing Company is part of the
Maxwell Communication Group of Companies.

Eye Openers ™

First published in Great Britain in 1992
by Dorling Kindersley Limited,
9 Henrietta Street, London WC2E 8PS

Reproduced by Colourscan, Singapore
Printed and bound in Italy by L.E.G.O., Vicenza

1 2 3 4 5 6 7 8 9 10

ISBN 0-689-71564-1

Library of Congress Catalog Card Number: 91-25688

tail wheel   propeller

landing
wheels

Passenger plane

This plane can carry nearly 400 people. It has four big engines. People travel to different places on passenger planes. The cabin crew gives safety instructions and makes sure the passengers are comfortable.

nose wheel

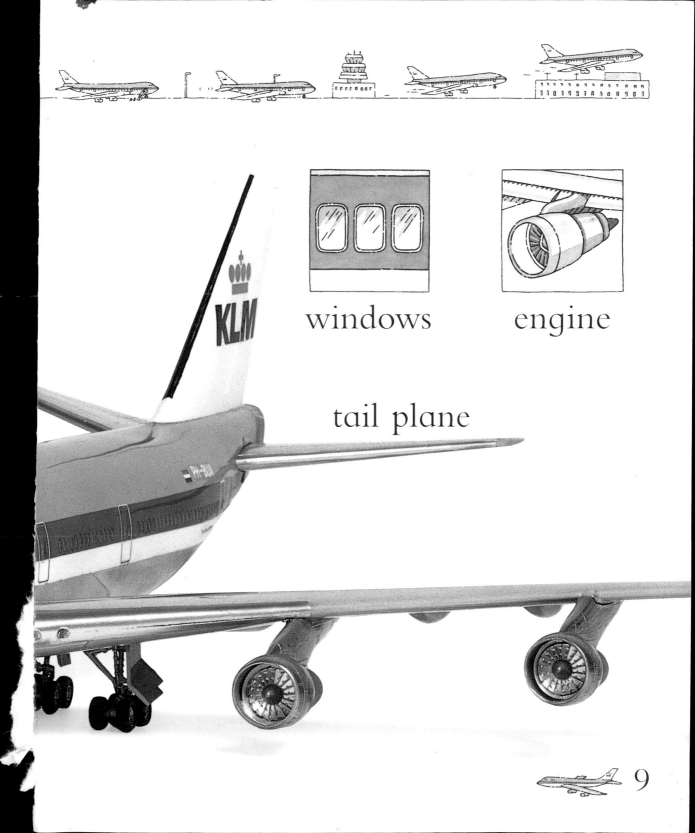

windows

engine

tail plane

9

Biplane

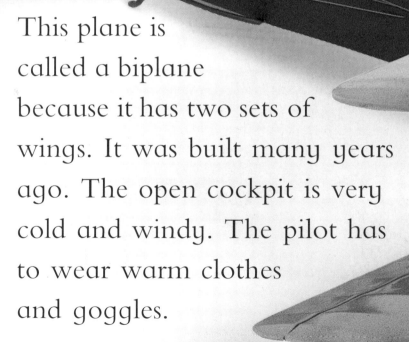

This plane is called a biplane because it has two sets of wings. It was built many years ago. The open cockpit is very cold and windy. The pilot has to wear warm clothes and goggles.

wing

rudder

propeller

wheel

Fighter plane

This fighter plane can shoot down enemy planes with its missiles. It also hits targets on the ground with its bombs. Fighter planes fly very fast. In an emergency, the pilot can escape by using the ejection seat.

nose

ejection
seat

missile

 13

Seaplane

wing

This plane can take off and land on water. It has floats instead of wheels. Its wings stay clear of the waves. Because seaplanes land on water, they can carry people to small islands. Seaplanes can't take off or land in rough weather.

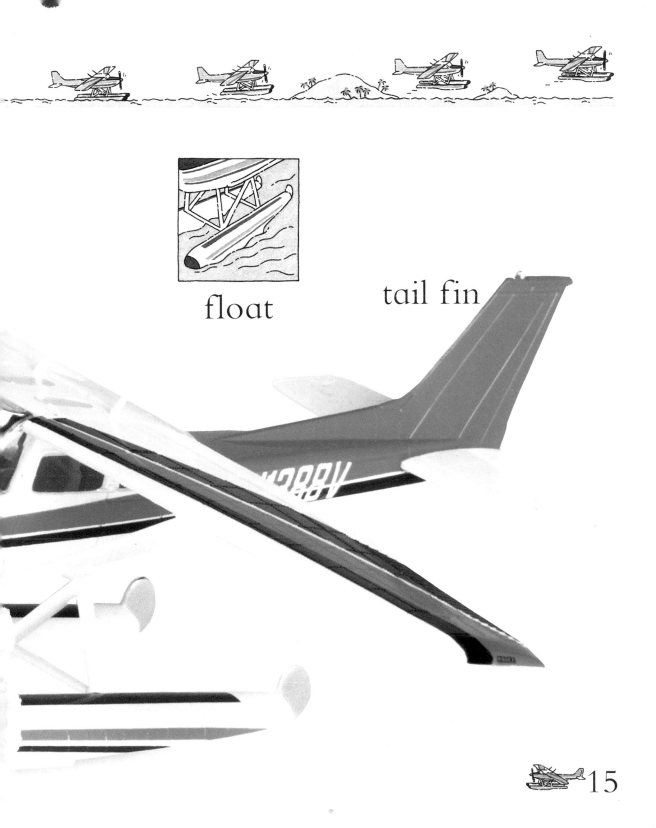

float

tail fin

15

Rescue helicopter

A helicopter's rotor blades
spin around and lift it
straight off the ground.
This helicopter is used to
rescue people. It can hover
in the air while the person
is pulled up by a winch.

XZ597

16

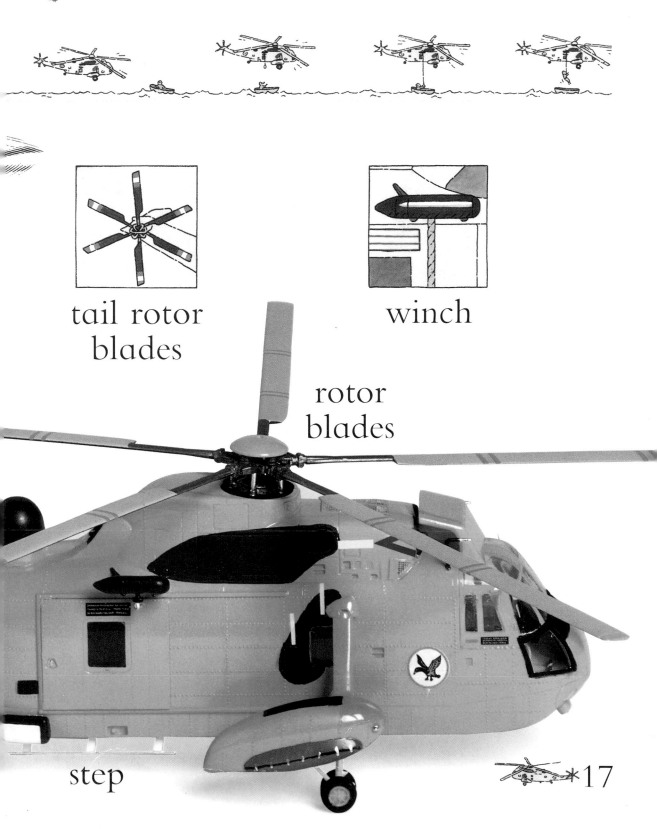

tail rotor
blades

winch

rotor
blades

step

Glider

rudder

KI

A glider's long wings help
it to fly. It doesn't have an engine,
so another plane tows it into the
sky. Then the glider pilot pulls
a lever, and the tow cable
falls away. People fly
gliders for fun.

18

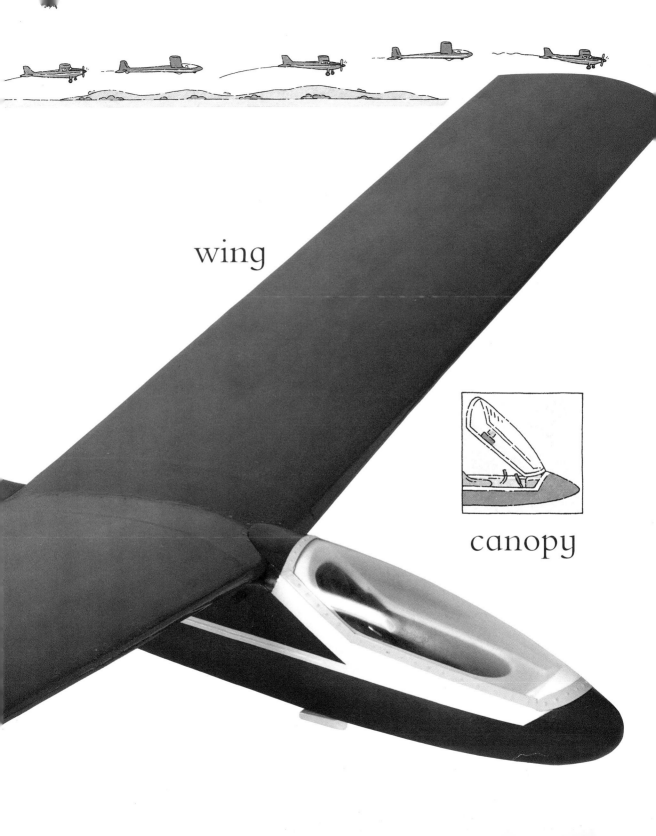

wing

canopy

Concorde

The Concorde is the
fastest passenger plane in the
world. It can travel faster than
the speed of sound. Its long, pointed
nose and turbojet engines help it to
fly fast. The nose drops down when
the plane takes off and lands to give
the pilot a clear view of the runway.

nose

passenger
door

turbojet
engine

tail fin

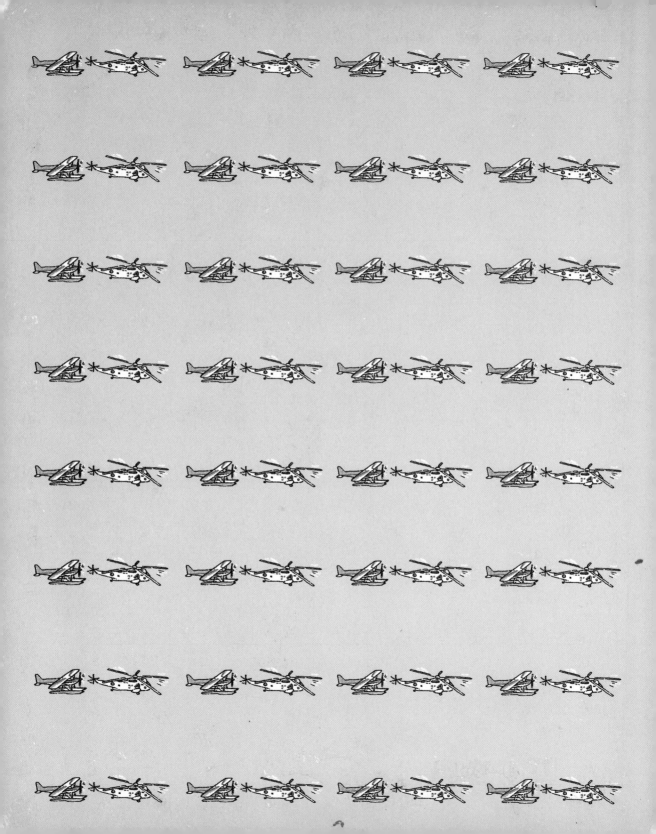